Written by **Tim McCanna**   Illustrated by **Jorge Martin**

BOING!

A Very Noisy ABC

xz
M

A PAULA WISEMAN BOOK
Simon & Schuster Books for Young Readers
New York London Toronto Sydney New Delhi

JINGLE-
JINGLE-
JINGLE!

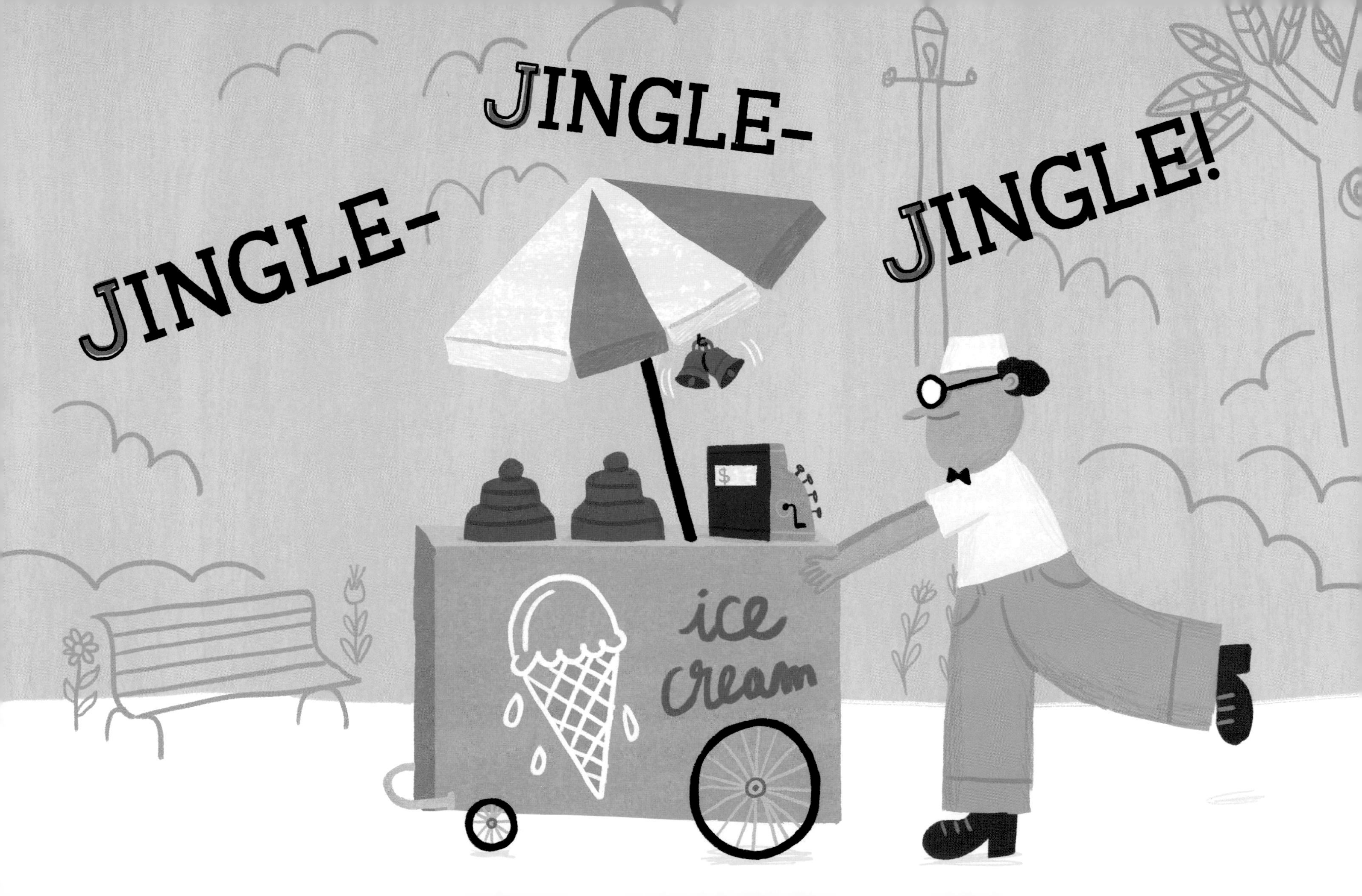

"Meow!"

"Ribbit! Ribbit!"

"Whew!"

"ZZZZzzzzz."

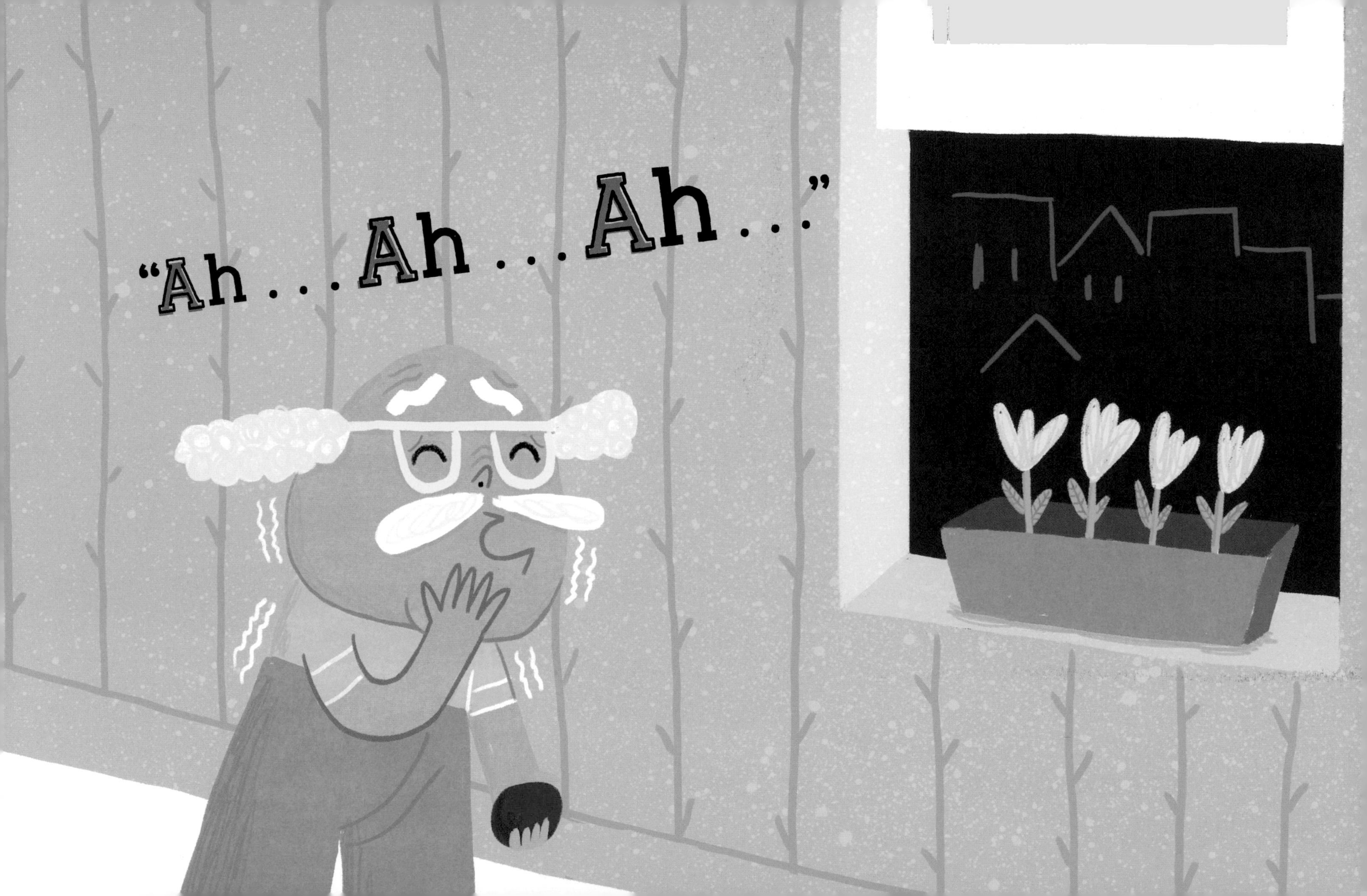

"Ah . . . Ah . . . Ah . . ."

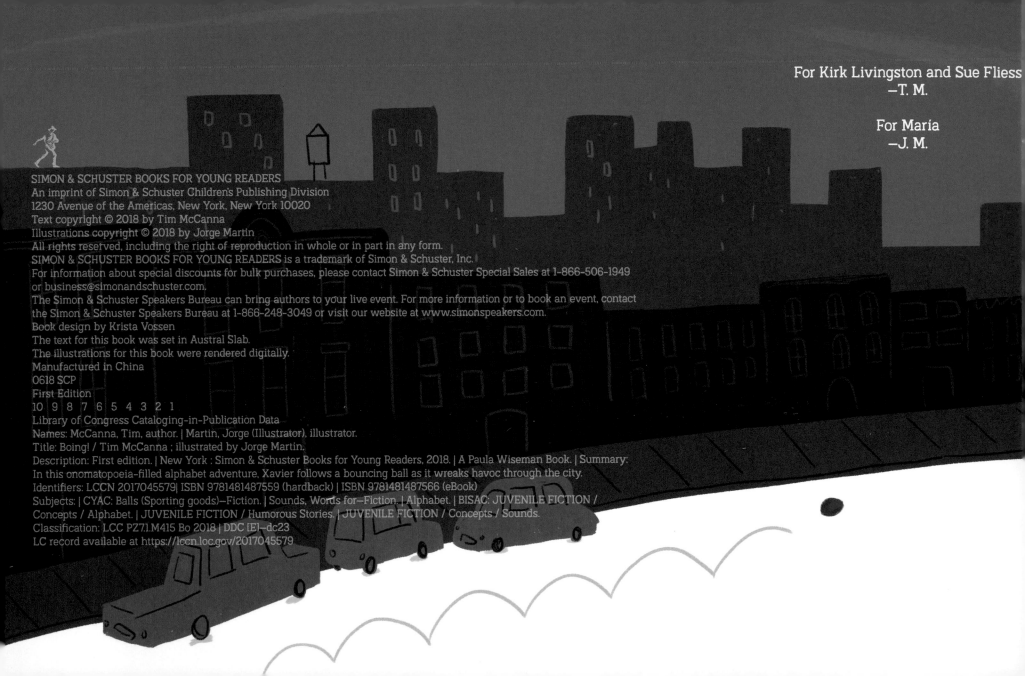

For Kirk Livingston and Sue Fliess
—T. M.

For Maria
—J. M.

SIMON & SCHUSTER BOOKS FOR YOUNG READERS
An imprint of Simon & Schuster Children's Publishing Division
1230 Avenue of the Americas, New York, New York 10020
Text copyright © 2018 by Tim McCanna
Illustrations copyright © 2018 by Jorge Martin
SIMON & SCHUSTER BOOKS FOR YOUNG READERS is a trademark of Simon & Schuster, Inc.
For information about special discounts for bulk purchases, please contact Simon & Schuster Special Sales at 1-866-506-1949
or business@simonandschuster.com.
The Simon & Schuster Speakers Bureau can bring authors to your live event. For more information or to book an event, contact
the Simon & Schuster Speakers Bureau at 1-866-248-3049 or visit our website at www.simonspeakers.com.
Book design by Krista Vossen
The text for this book was set in Austral Slab.
The illustrations for this book were rendered digitally.
Manufactured in China
0618 SCP
First Edition
10 9 8 7 6 5 4 3 2 1
Library of Congress Cataloging-in-Publication Data
Names: McCanna, Tim, author. | Martin, Jorge (Illustrator), illustrator.
Title: Boing! / Tim McCanna ; illustrated by Jorge Martin.
Description: First edition. | New York : Simon & Schuster Books for Young Readers, 2018. | A Paula Wiseman Book. | Summary:
In this onomatopoeia-filled alphabet adventure, Xavier follows a bouncing ball as it wreaks havoc through the city.
Identifiers: LCCN 2017045579| ISBN 9781481487559 (hardback) | ISBN 9781481487566 (eBook)
Subjects: | CYAC: Balls (Sporting goods)—Fiction. | Sounds, Words for—Fiction. | Alphabet. | BISAC: JUVENILE FICTION /
Concepts / Alphabet. | JUVENILE FICTION / Humorous Stories. | JUVENILE FICTION / Concepts / Sounds.
Classification: LCC PZ7.1.M415 Bo 2018 | DDC [E]—dc23
LC record available at https://lccn.loc.gov/2017045579